Wishes really do come true

Lucky Stars

Lucky Star that shines so bright,
Who will need your help tonight?
Light up the sky, it's thanks to you
Wishes really do come true . . .

Lucky Stars

Explore the sparkling world of the stars at
www.luckystarsbooks.co.uk

Wishes really do come true

Lucky Stars

The Ballerina Wish

Phoebe Bright

Illustrated by Karen Donnelly

MACMILLAN CHILDREN'S BOOKS

A Working Partners book

Special thanks to Maria Faulkner

First published 2012 by Macmillan Children's Books

This edition published 2013 by Macmillan Children's Books
a division of Macmillan Publishers Limited
20 New Wharf Road, London N1 9RR
Basingstoke and Oxford
Associated companies throughout the world
www.panmacmillan.com

ISBN 978-1-4472-0253-0

1 3 5 7 9 8 6 4 2

A CIP catalogue record for this book is available from
the British Library.

Printed and bound by CPI Group (UK) Ltd, Croydon CR0 4YY

With thanks to all the magical people in my life
for their belief in me

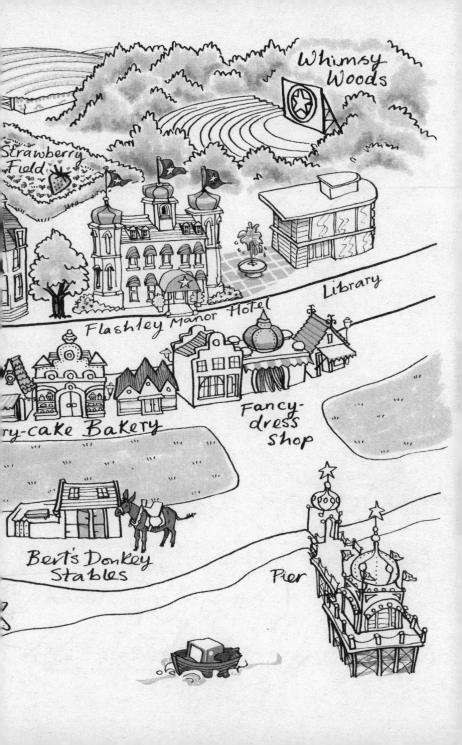

Contents

Hello, friend!

I'm Stella Starkeeper and I
want to tell you a secret. Have
you ever gazed up at the stars and
thought how magical they looked?
Well, you're right. Stars really do
have magic!

Their precious glittering light
allows me to fly down from the sky,
all the way to Earth. You see, I'm
always on the lookout for boys and
girls who are especially kind and
helpful. I train them to become
Lucky Stars - people who can make
wishes come true!

So the next time you're under the twinkling night sky, look out for me. I'll be floating among the stars somewhere. Do give me a wave!

Love from
Stella x

1
Crystal Gifts

Cassie looked at Alex's suitcase. It was overflowing with seaside toys, pebbles from the beach and brightly coloured sticks of rock. Alex picked up his microscope and tried to squeeze it in.

'It won't fit,' he groaned.

'Here's one more thing for you to pack,' Cassie said.

She held out a photo album with 'Alex's Holiday' written on the front. For the last

two weeks, Alex and his family had been
staying at Starwatcher Towers, the bed and
breakfast run by Cassie's parents. But now
his holiday was over.

'The album's full of special memories,'
she said, trying to smile.

Alex nodded and cleared his throat. He
smiled back, but Cassie knew he was sad.
Even Comet, his little white puppy, had his
ears down.

Alex opened the photo album and Cassie
pointed to one of the pictures.

'That's the view from Dad's observatory,'
she said. 'You can see the whole of Astral-
on-Sea from there.'

Cassie's dad was an astronomer and
at night he watched the stars from his

observatory. In the daytime, the observatory gave a spectacular view of the town and the seaside.

Alex flicked over the page and chuckled. There was a picture of Twinkle, Cassie's

old tom cat, and Comet chasing a ball.

'They're such good friends,' Cassie said.

'Just like us,' Alex replied. 'I wished for a friend and you became my best friend ever.'

'Your wish was the first one I helped to come true,' Cassie said. 'And you're the

only person who knows about my magic charms.'

They looked at Cassie's pretty charm bracelet. Every time she granted someone's wish she received another charm. So far, she had six charms that each gave her a magical power. The bird meant she could fly, the crescent moon allowed her

to talk to animals, the butterfly let her stop time, the flower made things appear and she had the power of invisibility thanks to the cupcake charm.

I still need to find out what power my new heart charm gives me, Cassie thought.

'You only need to get one more charm now,' said Alex. 'Then you'll be a Lucky Star and make wishes come true!'

Cassie sighed. 'If only you could stay and help me.'

She blinked away a tear. She couldn't imagine waking up tomorrow and not seeing Alex.

'Thanks for the photo album,' Alex said.

'You're welcome,' Cassie whispered.

Just then Alex's mum popped her head

round the bedroom door.
She noticed the bulging
suitcase.

'I don't think you'll fit
anything else in there,
Alex,' she said. 'Why
don't I pack the microscope?'

Alex showed his mum the
photo album.

'That's lovely,' she said. 'Shall I
pack this as well?'

'No thanks. I'll carry it on my
lap in the car,' Alex answered.

'Well, we don't need to leave until
this evening, so you have the rest of the day
here,' his mum said. She took the bucket
and spade to her guest room to pack.

11

'Maybe I can help you earn your last charm today,' Alex said to Cassie.

'That would be brilliant!' Cassie replied.

Alex jigged from foot to foot. 'I've got something for you too,' he said shyly.

From the wardrobe, Alex lifted out a box marked 'Top Secret'.

Cassie opened it. Inside were test tubes filled with beautiful crystals. They twinkled in shades of green, orange, violet and red.

'Oh, Alex, they look like stars!' she exclaimed.

'I grew the crystals myself,' Alex said with a grin.

'Thank you so much,' said Cassie. 'I'll go and put them in a special place in my room. You finish packing then we'll do

12

something extra-fun for the last day of your holiday.'

Carefully, Cassie carried the crystals to her bedroom. She gave Alex's gift pride of place on the shelf next to the card she had made for her parents' wedding anniversary. The crystals looked perfect in her room with its glass-panelled ceiling, moon-shaped lamp and starry wallpaper.

Suddenly the crystals lit up, shimmering like a rainbow. Cassie looked through the window. High in the blue sky, zooming between the soft, white clouds, a familiar orb of light was heading straight towards her room.

Rushing to the lever on her bedroom wall, Cassie pulled it down and one of the glass panels in her ceiling swung open. Just in time! The fizzing orb spun in through the gap and landed with an explosion of starlight.

With a *whizz* and a *fizz* and a *zip-zip-zip*, the orb transformed into Stella Starkeeper. Her silvery dress shimmered above her glittery leggings and shiny boots.

Cassie gave her friend a big hug. It was

Stella who had given her the charm bracelet for her birthday two weeks ago. Now the little charms tinkled quietly.

'You only have to find one more wish to help make come true, and then you'll be a Lucky Star,' Stella said. 'And when you succeed you can grant wishes whenever you please – as long as you feel it's right.'

'Do you think I can do it?' Cassie asked.

Stella's velvety-blue eyes sparkled. 'I believe in you. Remember, I chose you because you like helping people and making them happy.'

Cassie gave a little twirl.

Stella smiled. 'But first you must prove you are ready by earning your final charm,' she said.

Cassie nodded.

'I can't wait to be a
Lucky Star,' she sighed.
'But I'm so sad that
Alex is leaving.
Look, he gave
me these lovely
crystals.'

'They're
beautiful,'
Stella said.
'Well, perhaps
my clue will cheer you up.' She touched
the little heart-shaped charm on Cassie's
bracelet, making it glow. 'The clue to the
power of this charm is: *memories are precious*.'

Cassie felt a warm glow in her heart.

'And I've got a special surprise for you,'
Stella said. 'When you become a Lucky
Star, I will grant three wishes you can use
just for yourself.'

Cassie's eyes widened. Another
wonderful gift!

Sparkles swirled around Stella.

'Don't forget, Cassie,' she said.
'Memories are precious . . .'

And then she was gone, leaving Cassie
wondering what the clue meant.

2
The Forgetful Ballerina

Tip-tap, swoosh!

The strange noise echoed down the hallway. Cassie peered out of the door.

Tip-tap, swoosh!

There it was again. The sound was coming from Dad's observatory.

Cassie ran to Alex's room.

'Alex!' she called softly.

'I'm just making sure that I've packed everything,' he said, opening the door.

'Listen,' said Cassie. 'Can you hear a strange noise coming from my dad's observatory?'

Alex listened. 'I deduce there's someone up there,' he said. 'But I don't think it's your dad.'

Quietly, they crept up the stairs to the observatory and peered through the half-open door. Under the huge domed roof they saw a girl about their age, dancing around the shiny telescopes. Her lips were curved into a soft smile and her long hair whirled out behind her.

'Who's that?' Alex whispered.

'Izzy Nichols,' Cassie replied. 'One of the new guests.'

Enchanted, they watched Izzy spin

around on pointed toes. When she danced, her floaty dress billowed like a colourful cloud. She didn't see Cassie and Alex watching until they burst into applause

21

as she twirled round again in a perfect pirouette.

Izzy blushed and gave a pretty curtsy.

'You're brilliant,' Cassie said.

'Thanks,' Izzy replied. 'But I have to practise a lot. Our summer school is putting on a ballet when I get back and I'm playing Cinderella.'

Izzy blushed again. Holding on to the back of the old leather chair, she turned both feet out and bent her knees, dipping elegantly down and up.

'You make that look so easy,' Cassie said.

'These bends are called pliés. They took me a long time to get right,' Izzy replied. 'I've got to learn the steps in the right order

22

and do them in time to the music. Like this.'

Cassie and Alex watched Izzy run across
the room on her tiptoes, bend,
run, leap and then
stop.

'No,
that's all
wrong,' Izzy
said with a
frown. 'Is it
a plié first or
a leap? Oh dear, the show's going to be a
disaster!'

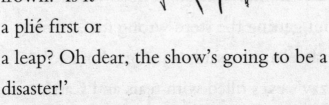

What a shame, Cassie thought. *I wonder if
my heart charm has the power to help?*

Just then, Izzy's mum came in. 'There
you are, Izzy,' she said. 'Hello, Cassie.'

'Hi,' Cassie replied. She'd met Mrs Nichols earlier. 'This is Alex. We've been watching Izzy dance – she's fantastic.'

'Very dedicated, just like a scientist,' Alex added.

'She practises every day at home,' said Mrs Nichols. 'But we're on holiday now, darling,' she told Izzy. 'You can relax and play.'

Izzy shook her head. 'I'm so worried about getting the steps wrong for Cinderella,' she said. 'I just can't relax.'

Izzy's eyes filled with tears and Cassie felt a lump in her own throat. Alex was leaving, and Izzy was unhappy . . . What a sad day!

Mrs Nichols gently wiped her daughter's

eyes with a tissue.
'I thought you
were worried,'
she said, 'so I've
found a summer
ballet class in
Astral-on-Sea.
It's a class for all
children, from
beginners to
experienced
dancers. It
should be fun.'

'I suppose,' said Izzy.

'It starts soon, so if you get changed
I'll drive you there,' said Mrs Nichols
with a kind smile. Then she disappeared

back down the stairs.

Izzy twisted the hem of her dress between her hands. 'There will be lots of people at the class I don't know,' she said quietly. 'That always makes me extra-nervous and forgetful. Oh, I wish I could remember my ballet routines!'

Cassie and Alex shared a secret smile. Izzy had made a wish.

She's the final person I have to help! Cassie thought, looking at her little heart charm, which was spinning like a dancer. *But how? And what magic power does this new charm have?*

Izzy was still frowning with worry. Cassie whispered an idea to Alex, who smiled and nodded.

To Izzy,
Cassie
suggested,
'How about
if Alex and I
come to the
ballet class too?
Then you won't be on your own.'

'You would be less nervous,' Alex added.

'And it's a scientific fact
that confidence helps
you concentrate.'

'Oh yes!
That's really kind
of you,' Izzy
replied, her face
lighting up.

They all clattered down the stairs. Izzy rushed to get ready while Alex followed Cassie to her bedroom.

'Er, I've just thought of another scientific fact,' Alex said to Cassie. 'I have two left feet! I'm not sure how useful I'll be in a ballet class.'

Poor Alex, Cassie thought. *It's the last day of his holiday, and a ballet class isn't exactly his idea of fun. But I need his help!*

Cassie remembered their adventure with Jacey Day, a pop singer who'd stayed at Starwatcher Towers. 'You were great as Jacey's backing singer, even though you didn't think you would be,' she told Alex. 'The dance steps you made up were brilliant!'

'That was fun,' Alex admitted. 'And I want to help Izzy – and help you earn your last charm. OK,' he agreed, smiling. 'I can't let my best friend down.'

Cassie gave him a big hug.

29

Just then, they heard a terrible screech from outside.

YEOWL! MEOW! YOWL!

Startled, Cassie and Alex looked at one another.

'Twinkle!' they both cried.

'Oh dear,' Cassie said. 'What can be wrong?'

3
Twinkle's Blanket

Cassie and Alex ran out to the back garden.

YEOWL! MEOW! YOWL!

'Now look here, mate,' Jamie the bin man was saying to Cassie's old tom cat. 'I can't have you ripping my bags open!'

Twinkle leaped on the bin bag Jamie was trying to put in the back of his truck, holding on tight with his claws.

'I'm so sorry,' said Cassie.

'That's all right, Cassie love,' Jamie replied. 'I've never seen him like this. It's like he doesn't want me to take the rubbish.'

'You can't get in Jamie's way like this, Twinkle,' Cassie said, scooping up her grumpy cat. 'I'll take him indoors so you can finish,' she added to Jamie.

'Thanks, young lady,' Jamie said. 'I hope he's OK.'

So do I, Cassie

thought. *I'll have to ask him what's wrong.*

Once in the kitchen, Cassie thought hard about her crescent-moon charm, which gave her the power to talk to animals. Silver sparkles swirled around her bracelet, over her cat and over Comet, who trotted along behind Alex.

'Oh, Twinkle. What's made you so cross?' she asked, stroking his head.

But Twinkle just yowled.

33

'Please tell me what's wrong,' Cassie said, hugging him as they walked into the hallway.

Cassie's mum popped her head round the dining-room door, where she had been tidying away the breakfast dishes.

'I think I know what's up with him,' Mum said, and pointed to the fluffy towel under the radiator – where Twinkle's blanket used to be. 'I had to throw that horrible blanket of his away,' she explained, wrinkling her nose. 'I could smell it even after I'd washed it!'

Once Mum had gone, Twinkle yowled, 'I loved my blanket!'

'I love this nice towel,' Comet yapped, sitting happily in the middle of it.

34

The Ballerina Wish

Twinkle leaped out of Cassie's arms, heading for the back door.

'Quick!' Cassie said to Alex. 'We've got to follow Twinkle!'

They hurried outside. Twinkle was running towards the orchard.

'He's going too fast for us to catch him,' said Alex with a groan.

But Cassie had an idea. She grabbed Alex's hand and thought hard about her bird charm. Her bracelet tingled as the magic began to work and her feet lifted off the ground. They flew after Twinkle, Comet running along behind.

At the bottom of the orchard was a wooden shed. Twinkle scrambled through a hole in the side. Cassie guided Alex back

to the ground, then pressed her nose against
the shed window. Inside, she could see a

grumpy Twinkle curled up on a pile of old sacks.

She tapped gently on the glass. 'Please come out, Twinkle,' she said.

'No,' Twinkle muttered. 'I don't feel wanted any more.'

Cassie looked pleadingly at Alex. 'I don't know how to cheer him up,' she said.

Alex held his puppy up to the window. 'Comet wants to play with you!' he called.

Comet wagged his tail. 'Come and chase leaves with me, Twinkle!' he barked.

But Twinkle just meowed sadly. 'Cats don't have much of their own,' he grumbled. 'My blanket was my favourite thing and now it's gone forever. So I'm staying in the shed!'

'Oh, Twinkle,' Cassie said. 'Mum didn't mean to upset you. Won't you get hungry in there?'

Twinkle laid his head on his paws. 'I'll never be hungry again,' he sniffed.

Alex put his arm round Cassie's shoulders. 'I know it's tough to leave Twinkle like this,' he said, 'but we've got a ballet class to go to. So put your best left foot forward!'

The Ballerina Wish

Alex's joke made Cassie smile and she
blew Twinkle a loving kiss.

'I'm going to help Izzy,' she told him.
'Then I'll come back and help you.'

Inside the B & B they found Dad in the
kitchen, polishing
the lens of one of
his telescopes.

He was listening to the weather forecast.

'*It will be a glorious afternoon followed by a cloudy night sky,*' the radio announcer was saying.

'Oh no,' Dad said.

'What's wrong, Dad?' Cassie asked.

'There's going to be a fantastic meteor shower tonight,' he explained. 'I thought Mum and I could watch it to celebrate our wedding anniversary. But it will be too cloudy to see anything in the sky!' With a sigh, he dropped the duster on to the table.

Cassie gave Dad a hug. What a shame!

So many things are going wrong today,

40

she thought. *Even if nothing else goes right,
I'm going to make sure Izzy's wish comes
true . . .*

4
Perfect Memory

'I'm so glad your parents let you come with me,' Izzy told Cassie and Alex as they climbed into the back of her mum's car.

'And we'll all be there to see you dance at the end of the class,' Mrs Nichols added.

Cassie and Alex were wearing shorts and T-shirts, but Izzy had on a leotard and tights.

'You look like a proper ballerina,' Cassie told her.

'Thanks,' Izzy said. She smiled, but Cassie noticed that she held her hands tightly together in her lap.

She's really worried, Cassie thought.

They drove down the hill and along the seafront, where holidaymakers were enjoying the sunshine. Further along the promenade, Cassie pointed out a reddish-brown building with tall windows.

'That's the Town Hall. It's where the ballet class is being held,' she said.

Mrs Nichols parked in a space outside the Town Hall. The other children attending the class were walking up the wide stone steps that led into the building. Cassie, Alex, Izzy and Mrs Nichols followed.

'Move!' a girl screeched.

44

The Ballerina Wish

Cassie's heart sank. She looked around to see a girl in a pink tutu and ballet shoes with ribbons wound about her ankles. The girl was spinning round, knocking into everyone else.

'Who's that?' Izzy whispered.

'Donna Fox,' Cassie replied. 'Her parents own Flashley Manor, the biggest hotel in Astral-on-Sea.'

'She tries to spoil everything,' Alex muttered.

They went through the doors and followed a sign that read, 'Ballet class – this way!' It directed them to a large hall with chairs round the edge and an MP3 player and speakers on a table.

'Come in, dancers!' a tall man said.

The Ballerina Wish

He wore black trousers and a white vest. Stretching out his arms in welcome, he moved gracefully towards them.

'I'm Roman, your teacher,' the man explained. 'Now, let's all learn some ballet and have lots of fun. At the end of the class, we'll do a performance for all the mums and dads!'

'Doesn't that sound wonderful?' Mrs Nichols said. She waved goodbye. 'See you later!'

Donna fluffed up the frilly layers of her tutu. 'I'm going to be the best dancer,' she boasted. 'I'm the best at everything.'

The other children were grinning excitedly too, but Cassie noticed Izzy looking around nervously.

'First, we must do some warm-up exercises,' Roman said. He switched on the MP3 player and the hall was filled with tinkling piano music. Roman lifted his arms upward. 'Pretend you want to touch the stars,' he said.

Cassie smiled. She knew what it felt like to touch a real star! All the children stretched their arms up like Roman showed them.

'And swing your feet,' Roman called.

As Cassie kicked her foot up, she saw

Izzy swing her foot high in the air and back again.

'Very good,' Roman said, nodding to Izzy.

Izzy blushed.

When the warm-up was finished, Roman paused the music. 'Excellent work,' he said. 'Now, if you've danced before, please come to the front of the class.'

'Mind out,' Donna snapped, pushing past Izzy

as she moved to the front.

'I bet she's never danced in her life,' Alex said crossly. 'Remember her terrible gym performance at Lia's birthday party?'

Izzy moved close to Cassie and Alex, her hands shaking. 'I think I'll stay with you,' she said.

Roman walked over to Cassie, Alex and Izzy, and the other children at the back. 'You can learn a lot from watching other dancers,' he told them. 'Just have fun and relax. You'll pick it up in no time!'

Then Roman pressed the play button on his MP3 player. Lovely music floated around them.

'Let's dance,' he said. 'Gallops, first!'

Cassie, Alex and Izzy galloped together. Alex neighed like a pony, making Izzy laugh.

'Now a leap,' Roman said. 'And then pirouette – which means spin.'

Together, they all leaped through the air
and twirled around.

'Well done,' Roman said. 'You're all
doing brilliantly. Next, I want you to try an
arabesque. That's a –'

Before Roman could explain, Izzy lifted
her leg behind her and stretched out her arms.

Cassie gasped. *She looks so elegant*, she
thought.

'Look, everyone,' Roman said. 'That is a
perfect arabesque.'

Izzy blushed again.

'And now let's do all the steps in order,'
Roman said.

Cassie noticed that Izzy did a neat gallop
and a leap, but forgot to spin before the
arabesque.

'Not so perfect
now, are you?'
Donna sneered.

Poor Izzy tried
again. But this time
she pirouetted at the
wrong moment,
bumping into Donna.

'Watch out, you
clumsy girl!' Donna said,
glaring at Izzy.

'I'm so s-sorry,' Izzy stammered.

'Don't worry about Donna,' Cassie said.
But Izzy looked as if she might cry. *I've got
to do something to make her wish come true,*
she thought. *But what? I can't remember the
routine either . . .*

Alex was repeating the steps quietly to himself. 'Gallop, leap, turn, arabesque,' he muttered.

Cassie was impressed. Although Alex's leg pointed to the front for the arabesque

instead of behind, he was doing everything in the right order.

Cassie whispered the steps too, concentrating hard to memorize the routine. Suddenly, she saw the heart charm glowing on her bracelet! Her heart raced with excitement, and she ducked behind one of the floor-length curtains that hung from the windows so no one would notice her.

A shower of glittering sparkles swirled
around her bracelet and over her feet. Still
hidden by the curtain, Cassie tried the
dance steps again in order. Amazed, she
found that now she could remember the
routine perfectly.

Stella said that memories are precious, she
thought, *and my heart charm gives me perfect
memory. Now I know how to help Izzy!*

5
Cinderella's Dance

Cassie danced out from behind the curtain and through the class of children, until she was in front of Izzy and Alex.

'We're going to use my magic heart charm to help Izzy remember the steps,' she told Alex quietly. To Izzy, she said, 'Just follow my moves!'

Izzy watched Cassie carefully then copied her sequence of steps. Cassie glanced over her shoulder and smiled. Her plan was

working! Izzy was dancing the routine
perfectly. She looked lovely, leaping high,
her toes pointed, and finally stretching her
arms in a graceful arabesque.

'Beautiful.' Roman called out to Izzy.
She didn't blush this time.
Her face beamed as she

danced around
the room, leaping,
twirling and
holding
the
arabesque
perfectly.
'Izzy's got it!' Cassie
said excitedly to
Alex.

Alex turned to watch Izzy. 'She's great!' he agreed.

Cassie glanced down at her charm bracelet hopefully, but her heart sank. She stopped dancing and moved to the side of the room.

'What's wrong?' Alex asked, following her.

'I thought I'd made Izzy's wish come true and earned my last charm,' Cassie said. 'But it hasn't appeared.'

She and Alex looked at one another. What had gone wrong?

Roman clapped his hands. The class danced to a halt, all except Donna who bumped into Roman.

'Take a little more care,' Roman said.

'It isn't a solo dance.'

Donna stomped off to the other side of the room, sulking.

The audience started arriving and the seats round the edge of the hall were soon packed. Cassie and Alex saw their parents, and Izzy waved excitedly to her mum.

'Are you OK?' Cassie asked her.

'I'm fine now,' Izzy replied with a smile as she practised the arabesque again. 'I

managed to dance that new
routine in front of a whole
class of strangers,
thanks to you. I've
never had so much
fun when I dance.
You two are magical!'

Roman clapped his hands again and the
children lined up. The music began and
Izzy galloped confidently across the room,
Cassie and Alex dancing along beside her.
When they got to the arabesque, Izzy's foot
was stretched high in the air.

Cassie noticed that Izzy had been dancing
so freely that her hair had come loose and
whirled around her, just as it had done in
the observatory. She looked happy and

danced beautifully. Cassie smiled. She had definitely granted Izzy's wish. So why hadn't she received the last charm?

The audience clapped as the dance came to an end. Then suddenly some new music came on the MP3 player. Roman had accidentally tapped the wrong button.

'Oops,' he said.

But Izzy carried on dancing, her feet spinning her across the floor. Cassie recognized the jumps and arm movements.

'I think that's her *Cinderella* routine,' she said to Alex. 'And look – she's not nervous at all.'

Izzy dipped and leaped, finishing with a pirouette, spinning on the spot so her

hair flew out around her.

She finished the dance, and everyone except Donna applauded loudly. Izzy glowed.

'I didn't worry about the steps. They just came naturally,' Izzy excitedly told Cassie and Alex. 'I was enjoying dancing too much.'

Izzy's mum walked over and joined them. She was beaming. 'That was fantastic! I'm so proud of you,' she said, hugging Izzy.

'She dances from her heart,' Roman said, coming to stand with them. 'Izzy, the audience will always love you when you dance with such joy.'

'I can't wait to perform in *Cinderella* now I know I can remember the steps,' said Izzy. 'And it's all thanks to both of you.' Izzy smiled at Cassie and Alex.

Cassie smiled back, but inside she

couldn't help feeling
disappointed. On
her wrist her bracelet
tingled in a strange
way, but her final
charm still hadn't
appeared.

I wonder why, she
thought. *Without my next charm, how will I
ever become a Lucky Star?*

6
A New Lucky Star

With a heavy heart Cassie stood in the hallway of Starwatcher Towers. The afternoon at the beach was over and Izzy had gone out with her mum, leaving Cassie and Alex to say goodbye.

Outside, Cassie could hear her mum and dad talking to Alex's parents.

'We've had such a wonderful time,' Alex's dad was saying. 'Astral-on-Sea is so much nicer than the busy city we're going

back to. We'll stop at the pier on the way home and take in the view for the last time.'

'Yes, it's a very relaxing place,' Alex's mum agreed. 'We wish we lived here.'

I wish you did too, thought Cassie. She glanced at Alex. His suitcase stood next to him, the photo album Cassie had given him balanced on top. He took his glasses off and polished them on his sleeve.

'I'm sorry you didn't get your final charm,' he whispered sadly. 'Then you could make Mum's wish come true.'

'At least we granted Izzy's wish,' Cassie replied.

Alex nodded and cleared his throat, popping his glasses back on.

The Ballerina Wish

'Can't seem to stop my glasses misting up,' Alex said.

Cassie knew Alex was trying not to cry. She felt the same.

'I'll miss you,' she said.

Alex nodded. 'I'll miss you too.'

Placing a paw on Cassie's knee, Comet gave a little whine.

MEOW!

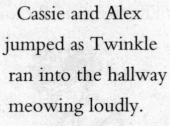

Cassie and Alex jumped as Twinkle ran into the hallway meowing loudly.

'He's come out of the shed!' Cassie said, stroking Twinkle behind the ears. 'I think he wants to say goodbye to Comet.'

She concentrated on her crescent-

moon charm. Silver sparkles swirled around her bracelet and over Twinkle and Comet.

'Comet likes that towel, so I want to give it to him to remember me by,' Twinkle meowed.

'That's very kind of you, Twinkle,' Cassie said.

Comet ran over to Twinkle and licked his ears.

'Thank you, thank you,' he barked.

'That's quite enough,' Twinkle grumbled, but Cassie could see that he was pleased. 'It's been very interesting to have a puppy friend. Now, I have to get back to my pile of sacks.'

Cassie translated for Alex.

'There are lots of scientific theories about friendship,' Alex said. 'You and I will be friends forever – that's my prediction.'

'We'll see one another again – I just know it,' Cassie whispered, hugging him.

'Well, goodbye for now,' Alex replied, squeezing her extra hard.

'Time to go now, love,' Alex's mum called.

Trying not to cry, Cassie followed Alex outside.

The Ballerina Wish

Alex and Comet got into the car, Alex clutching his photo album. Comet sat on the towel. Cassie stood next to her parents, waving to Alex and his parents as they drove slowly away.

A tear slid down her cheek. She pulled one of her pretty tissues decorated with stars from her pocket, and wiped her eyes.

Dad patted her shoulder gently.

'It's hard to say goodbye, isn't it?' said Mum. 'Come on, let's go inside.'

'I'd like to stay out here for a little while,' Cassie replied.

'OK,' Mum said, kissing the top of Cassie's head on her way into the house. 'Come in when you're ready.'

Cassie sat on the doorstep. It was such a sad day: Twinkle hiding in the shed, Alex going home and no sign of her last charm.

But at least I have all my precious memories,

74

Stella raised her wand and filled the bedroom with tiny glittering stars.

'I am so proud of you, Cassie,' she said, kissing Cassie on the cheek.

'But I've let you down,' Cassie said sadly. She held the pretty bracelet up for Stella to see. 'I didn't earn my last charm.'

'Oh, but you did,' Stella explained. 'You helped Izzy's wish come true, didn't you? It's just that this charm is so special I want to give it to you myself.'

Stella unclipped a star-shaped charm from the bracelet on her own wrist and attached it to Cassie's. It was a tiny version of the star on the top of Stella's wand.

Stella touched the new charm with

her wand and a shower of tiny glittering
stars fluttered over Cassie.

Cassie felt like jumping up and down
with joy. She had done it after all! But then
she glanced at Alex's shining crystals and
remembered that he wasn't here to share
the excitement.

I'll have to write and tell him, she thought
sadly.

'Congratulations, Cassie,' said Stella.
'You've always watched and listened for
someone to make a wish – someone who
really deserved your help. And now that
you're a Lucky Star you can grant wishes
any time.' She smiled. 'Now it's your turn
to make three wishes.'

What will I wish for? Cassie thought,

79

looking up at the cloudy night sky. And then she realized. *I know just what my first wish will be . . .*

7
Cassie's Three Wishes

Whoosh!

Hand in hand, Stella and Cassie flew
through the open window of Cassie's
bedroom. Light as balloons, they
circled over Starwatcher Towers. In the
observatory, Cassie could see Dad shaking
his head sadly.

'What will your first wish be?' Stella
asked.

'It's my mum and dad's wedding

anniversary. Dad was really excited because there's supposed to be a meteor shower tonight,' Cassie explained. 'But it's too cloudy to see it. I'd like to make their anniversary absolutely perfect.'

'Make your wish,' Stella said.

Cassie thought hard about the star-shaped charm.

'I wish the dark clouds would go away,' she said.

Silvery stardust swirled from the charm and out across the night sky. The dark clouds scudded away.

Delighted, Cassie watched Dad's face break into a grin and Mum walk into the observatory carrying the card Cassie had made them. Dad pointed at the glorious

night sky, twinkling with starlight.

Cassie and Stella flew quickly into the back garden, so they wouldn't be seen.

Then Cassie spotted Twinkle through the shed window, sitting sadly on the pile of sacks. 'I know what my second wish is!' she said with a grin.

Cassie thought hard about her star-shaped charm again.

'I wish Twinkle would understand how much we love him,' she said.

Silvery stardust swirled around her bracelet and over the garden. A trail of Twinkle's favourite treats appeared, leading from the scratchy sacks, out of the shed and into Starwatcher Towers. Cassie and Stella flew from window to

window, watching him go.

Happily munching, Twinkle followed the treats all the way to Cassie's room.

'Look,' Cassie said to Stella as they gazed down through the glass ceiling. 'Twinkle's got a brand-new cat basket with his name written on the side.'

'And there are gorgeous, soft blankets inside,' Stella said.

Cassie thought hard about her crescent-

84

moon charm. Sparkles swirled over her wrist and through the open window to Twinkle.

'I hope you like your new basket, Twinkle,' Cassie said.

'I love it,' Twinkle purred, settling down on the blankets. 'And I love you, Cassie!'

Cassie chuckled and blew Twinkle a kiss.

'You have one more wish left,' Stella said.

Cassie smiled. She knew exactly what she was going to wish for.

It's a very big wish, she thought, a little nervously. *I wonder if it's too big to come true.*

She led Stella high above the promenade and along the sands where the waves were moving in and out with the tide. On they

flew, over the Pier Theatre and the Town
Hall, above Flashley Manor Hotel and the
Fairy-cake Bakery. Finally they stopped at
the pier. Alex's car was just driving away,
leaving Astral-on-Sea behind.

Cassie flew quickly, following the road out of the town.

But would the wish work? she wondered.

Cassie concentrated really hard on her star-shaped charm. She remembered that Alex's mum had wished she lived in Astral-on-Sea and how much Alex's dad had enjoyed his stay. Most of all, she thought about Alex and how he'd become her best friend.

'I wish Alex and his mum and dad lived in Astral-on-Sea,' she said.

The silver sparkles swirled around her bracelet and then showered the roof of the car. Cassie held her breath.

The car slowed and pulled over. Cassie's heart beat faster. She and Stella flew closer

and hid behind a hedge so they wouldn't be seen. Through the car window Cassie could see Alex leaning forward to listen to his parents.

'I don't want to leave this lovely seaside town,' his mum was saying.

'Neither do I,' his dad agreed. 'I could stay here forever.'

'Let's live at Starwatcher Towers!' Alex piped up from the back seat.

'We can't live at a B & B, love,' his mum said.

Outside, Cassie watched nervously. Would they drive away?

Alex's dad looked first at Alex's mum and then at Alex.

'Are we all sure this is where we want

to live?' he asked.

'Yes, yes, yes! Please,' Alex begged.

His mum nodded. 'I can't think of anywhere else I'd rather be,' she said.

'That settles it,' his dad said, smiling. 'We'll stay at Starwatcher Towers until we find a place of our own in Astral-on-Sea.'

Cassie's heart soared. Her wish had been granted! This was

the most wonderful day ever!

Once Alex's dad had turned the car round to head back to the town, Cassie and Stella flew home. They dropped gently though the open panel into Cassie's bedroom. Twinkle meowed softly from his new bed.

Cassie put her arms round Stella and gave her a huge hug. 'Thank you for helping me to become a Lucky Star,' she said.

90

'It was all your hard work, Cassie,' Stella replied. 'And now that you're a Lucky Star you'll be able to help many more people.'

With a shower of sparkles, Stella disappeared.

On Cassie's wrist all seven charms tinkled together.

I wonder whose wish I'll grant next? Cassie thought.

'There you are, darling,' said Mum, putting her head round the bedroom door. 'Dad and I are going outside to watch the meteor shower. Do you want to come?'

'Yes, please,' Cassie said, her eyes shining. She pulled on her coat and ran downstairs.

Cassie stood between her mum and dad. Overhead, the first meteors streaked

silvery trails across the night sky.

'Magical,' breathed Cassie.

In the distance, a car's headlights appeared, weaving up the road towards the B & B.

'That looks like Alex's car,' Dad said. 'They're coming back!'

Cassie gave a whoop of excitement. She couldn't wait to show Alex her new charm.

High above, one special star shone extra brightly.

'See you soon, Stella,' Cassie murmured. 'I wonder what my next adventure will be?'

Cassie's Things to Make and Do!

Join in the Lucky Stars fun!

The Ballerina Wish Wordsnake

I'm so happy now that I'm a Lucky Star! Can you help me find the words listed below? The words go in one continuous line. The line can go forwards, backwards, up or down but it never goes diagonally. I've found the first one for you!

CRYSTALS

STELLA

BALLET

IZZY

CHARM

MAGICAL

Start
↓

C R Y L

A T S A

L S S C

L E T I

L A B G

L L A A

E R M M

T A H C

I Z Z Y

Cassie's Lucky Star Decorations

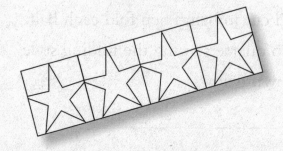

I'm sure you have seen those pretty, joined-up paper chains. Well, I'm going to teach you how to make a Lucky Star paper chain. You can ask a grown-up to help you.

You will need:

A piece of A4 paper

A pen

A pair of scissors

1. Fold the paper in half, lengthways, and cut in half. Then fold each half into quarters, using the folding style shown below.

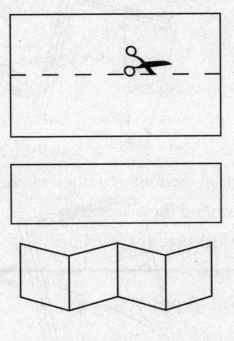

2. With a pencil draw an outline of a star shape on to the top face of your paper, make sure the two points of your star that touch the edges of the folds don't end in a sharp point – just like this!

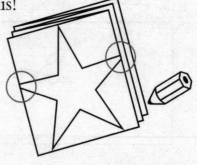

3. Keeping the folds together, carefully cut around the star shape you have drawn.

★ 4. Unfold the paper to reveal your very own magical star paper chain. Do the same with the other half of the paper.

To make a longer chain you can use a larger piece of paper or alternatively you can use sticky tape to connect your two chains together.

Cassie's Top Tip:
Why not write your wishes on to the centre of the stars. Remember, wishes really do come true!

Answers

Don't look unless
you're really stuck!

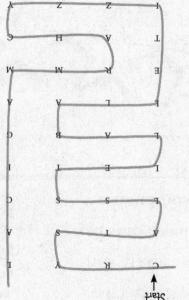

Start →

The Ballerina Wish
Wordsnake

While Cassie was training to be a Lucky Star she made lots of new friends. You'll meet them all too in the Lucky Stars stories!

Cassie

Alex

Comet

Twinkle

Stella

Sita

Sunbeam

Jacey

Marcus

Roxy

Izzy

The Best Friend Wish

Phoebe Bright

With a whizz, fizz
and pop, magical Stella
Starkeeper appears and tells
Cassie she will be a Lucky Star –
someone who can grant wishes.
Could Alex, her new friend,
have a secret wish?

The Perfect Pony Wish

Phoebe Bright

Sunbeam the pony has
run away! Cassie must help
a little girl's wish come true and
find him before the showjumping
competition begins. Will
Sunbeam be the perfect pony?

The Pop Singer Wish

Phoebe Bright

Pop sensation
Jacey Day is performing
in Astral-on-Sea, but her
backing singers are ill! Jacey
wishes someone could fix things . . .
Cassie must find a way for
the show to go on!

The Birthday Wish

Phoebe Bright

Lia has a cake
disaster at her party!
What this birthday really needs
is a sprinkling of Lucky Star magic . . .
Can Cassie make a special
birthday wish come true?

Wishes really do come true

Lucky Stars

Explore the magical world of Lucky Stars!

For fun things to make and do – as well as games and quizzes – go to:

www.luckystarsbooks.co.uk

Wishes really do come true
Lucky Stars

Cassie is training to become a Lucky Star –
someone who can make wishes come true!
Follow her on more exciting adventures as
she meets new friends in need of help.